Mystery
at the
Big Blue House

by Janelle Cherrington
based on a teleplay by P. Kevin Strader
illustrated by Tom Brannon

Simon Spotlight

New York   London   Toronto   Sydney   Singapore

Based on the TV series *Bear in the Big Blue House*™
created by Mitchell Kriegman. Produced by
The Jim Henson Company for Disney Channel.

SIMON SPOTLIGHT
An imprint of Simon & Schuster Children's Publishing Division
1230 Avenue of the Americas
New York, New York 10020
SIMON SPOTLIGHT and colophon are registered trademarks of
Simon & Schuster.
Manufactured in the United States of America
First Edition   10 9 8 7 6 5 4 3 2 1
ISBN 0-689-83339-3

It was a strange day at the Big Blue House. Everywhere Bear turned, things were disappearing!

"I think we have a real mystery on our hands," Bear announced.

It all started at the otter pond. Pip and Pop were playing with some sticks, when they stopped to ask Bear some questions.

Then, all of a sudden, Pip yelled, "Our sticks!"

"What's wrong, guys?" Bear asked.

"They were right here," said Pip.

"And now they're gone," exclaimed Pop.

"That's strange," said Bear. "I don't see them anywhere, either."

"It's mysterious, all right," said Pop.

"Oh, well," said Pip. "I guess we'll have to go get some new ones. See you later, Bear."

"Bye, guys," Bear said as he turned to go back to the house. "Good luck."

Strange things were happening in the kitchen, too.

Ojo was playing dress-up and had just taken off her hat when Bear came inside.

"Hi, Bear," she said.

"Hi, Ojo," Bear replied. "That's a nice ribbon on your hat."

"Thanks, Bear," said Ojo. "I like it too."

Meanwhile, Tutter had just finished hanging his laundry by the window to dry, when something caught his attention.

"Uh, Bear, did you hear something?" he asked.

"No. What kind of sound did you hear?" Bear replied.

"I heard it, Tutter!" Ojo exclaimed. "It sounded like a whistling and—Hey! What happened to the ribbon on my hat?"

"And my blue towel," Tutter added, pointing to the empty spot on his clothesline. "My towel is gone too! It was right there, right there I tell you!"

"You know," said Bear, "mysterious things are happening everywhere today. Pip and Pop's sticks disappeared from the otter pond before. Let's keep our eyes open and be on the lookout."

"We'll do better than that, Bear," Ojo announced. "Detective Tutter LeMouse, and I, Detective Ojo, will look for clues."

"Yeah, Bear," Tutter said, holding up a magnifying glass with a flourish. "The Big Blue House Detectives are on the case! We will begin by returning to the scene of the crime—the window!"

"That's right," said Bear. "Both the towel and the hat were by the window. That's pretty good detective work, guys. Maybe we should look around the window."

They looked, and they all spotted something at once.

"Look, a clue!" cried Ojo.

"It's a feather," said Bear. "Who would leave a feather by the window?"

"Treelo likes feathers, doesn't he?" Ojo asked excitedly.

"Treelo has a feather *collection*," Tutter declared. "And he likes to whistle *and* swing through windows!"

"Maybe we'd better go ask Mr. Treelo A. Lemur some questions," Ojo said.

So they all headed up to Bear's bedroom. Just as they suspected, Treelo was there. He was holding an empty box.

"Hey, Treelo!" Bear said. "We're trying to solve a mystery today and we are hoping that you can help us."

"Okay," Treelo began. "But—" Treelo tried to show everyone his empty box, but Tutter interrupted.

"Is it true, Mr. Treelo, that you like feathers?" Tutter asked.

"Yes. Treelo like feathers," Treelo answered.

"Aha!" said Ojo. "And isn't it also true that you like to swing in windows and that you like to whistle?"

"Yes, Treelo like that, but—" Treelo said as he held up his empty box again.

"Just as we suspected," Tutter declared. "We have one more question for you. Isn't it true that this feather we found in the kitchen window, where my towel and Ojo's hat ribbon were before they disappeared, is from *your* feather collection?"

"Nope," said Treelo. "Treelo's feathers missing too, see?"

"*What?*" asked Ojo and Tutter. They were stunned.

"Treelo, where did you find your empty feather box?" Bear asked.
Treelo pointed to the open bedroom window.

"Another open window, eh?" Tutter said as he climbed up on the windowsill. "Bear, I think I see more feathers down there!"

"Yeah, I see them too," Ojo said. "It looks like a trail of feathers . . ."

". . . leading straight to the otter pond," said Tutter and Ojo at the same time.

So they all went outside to follow the trail of clues leading from the Big Blue House to the otter pond.

"That's Treelo's feather," Treelo said a few times along the way.

The trail of feathers led them straight to a tree.

"Wait a minute," Ojo said. "I hear whistling again. I think it's another clue."

The whistling sounded like it was coming from right above them!

"It's our friend Mr. Woodpecker!" Bear declared.

Mr. Woodpecker was very busy building a nest. What was he using?

"My ribbon!" said Ojo.

"My feathers!" said Treelo.

"Pieces of my towel!" said Tutter.

"Hi, guys," said Pop, popping up out of nowhere.

"Look, Pop," said Pip. "Our sticks are up there in the nest too."

"It sure looks nice and cozy," said Bear with a chuckle.

Bear turned to look at Tutter and Ojo.

"Well, guys, it looks like you cracked the case," he said.

"Ah, yes," Ojo began. "Another mystery solved by Detective Ojo . . ."

". . . and Tutter LeMouse, Big Blue House Detectives!" Tutter finished.